For Alvie and Ted,

and many thanks to David, Deirdre, and Daniel

Text copyright © 2007 by Allan Ahlberg
Illustrations copyright © 2007 by Bruce Ingman

First U.S. edition 2007

Library of Congress Cataloging-in-Publication Data
Ahlberg, Allan.
Previously / Allan Ahlberg ; Bruce Ingman. —1st U.S. ed.
p.    cm.
Summary:  The adventures of various nursery rhyme and fairy tale characters are retold in backward sequence with each tale interrelated to the other. Includes Goldilocks, Jack and the beanstalk, Jack and Jill, the frog prince, Cinderella, and the gingerbread man.
ISBN 978-0-7636-3542-8
[1. Characters in literature—Fiction.  2. Fairy tales.
3. Humorous stories.]    I. Ingman, Bruce, date, ill.  II. Title.
PZ7.A2688Pre  2007
[E]—dc22        2006051831

10 9 8 7 6 5 4 3 2 1

Printed in China

This book was typeset in Shinn Light.
The illustrations were done in acrylic.

Candlewick Press
2067 Massachusetts Avenue
Cambridge, Massachusetts 02140

visit us at www.candlewick.com

Pre

# viously

CANDLEWICK PRESS
CAMBRIDGE, MASSACHUSETTS

Allan Ahlberg • Bruce Ingman

Goldilocks arrived home
all bothered and hot.

Previously she had been
running like mad in the dark woods.

Previously she had been
climbing out of somebody else's window.

Previously she had been
sleeping in somebody else's bed,
eating somebody else's porridge,
and breaking somebody else's chair!

Previously she had been humming a tune
and having a little skip by herself in the dark woods.

Previously she had bumped into
a hurtling and older boy named . . .

# Jack

Jack was running like mad
in the dark woods
with a hen under his arm.

Previously he had stolen the hen
and climbed down a beanstalk.

Previously he had crept out of
an enormous house.
through an enormous cat door.

Previously he had been
hiding in an enormous shoe.

Previously he had
climbed *up* the beanstalk.

Previously he had swapped his cow
for some magic beans.

Previously his unhappy
(not to say desperate) mother
had sent him to market to sell the cow
because they were so poor.

Previously he had been
playing soccer with his little pals.

Previously he had come tumbling down
the high hill
with his argumentative little sister . . .

# Jill

Jill and Jack had been
climbing the hill with a bucket.

Previously they had been
arguing over who should carry the bucket,
who had carried the bucket last time,
and, anyway, where *was* the bucket?

Previously, while eating their breakfast
and arguing over the free gift
in the cornflakes box,
they had been said "Hello!" to
through the open kitchen window
by a small green . . .

# Frog

The Frog was sitting on the windowsill
with a sorrowful look in his eye
and a crown on his head.

Previously he had been . . .

# A Prince

The Prince was a sorrowful young man.

Previously a wicked fairy
had put a spell on him.

Previously he had been
a cheerful young man,
eating his dinner from golden plates
and traveling his kingdom
in a milk–white Mercedes.

Previously he had fallen in love
with a disappearing girl named . . .

# Cinderella

Cinderella was running like mad
away from the ball.

Previously she had been dancing
her socks off with the Prince.

Previously a *good* fairy
had put a spell on *her*.

Previously she had been
dressed in rags
and slaving away for the Ugly Sisters.

Previously, on her afternoon off
and out for a stroll in the dark woods,
*she* had been bumped into by . . .

# The Gingerbread Boy

The Gingerbread Boy was being chased by
a little old man,
a little old woman,
a cow (a different cow),

a horse,
a butcher,
a baker,
a schoolful of children,
and a quick brown fox.

Previously he had been
baked in an oven.

Previously he had been
a bag of flour
on a shelf
in a shop,
a field of golden wheat,
a sackful of seeds.

Previously the Farmer (Goldilocks's uncle)
had plowed the ground
and planted the seeds,
reaped and sowed,
sowed and reaped.

And previously Goldilocks herself
and Jack and Jill
and all the others,
even the little old man
and the little old woman,
had all been tiny babies . . .
previously.

And all the bears were cubs.
And all the frogs were tadpoles.
And all the buckets and chairs
and ballroom floors
were planks of wood.
And all the wood was trees
in the dark woods.

In the sun and the wind and the rain,
under the endless sky,
once upon a time . . .

Previously.